A Note to Parents and Teachers

Kids can imagine, kids can laugh and kids can learn to read with this exciting new series of first readers. Each book in the Kids Can Read series has been especially written, illustrated and designed for beginning readers. Humorous, easy-to-read stories, appealing characters, and engaging illustrations make for books that kids will want to read over and over again.

To make selecting a book easy for kids, parents and teachers, the Kids Can Read series offers three levels based on different reading abilities:

Level 1: Kids Can Start to Read

Short stories, simple sentences, easy vocabulary, lots of repetition and visual clues for kids just beginning to read.

Level 2: Kids Can Read with Help

Longer stories, varied sentences, increased vocabulary, some repetition and visual clues for kids who have some reading skills, but may need a little help.

Level 3: Kids Can Read Alone

Longer, more complex stories and sentences, more challenging vocabulary, language play, minimal repetition and visual clues for kids who are reading by themselves.

With the Kids Can Read series, kids can enter a new and exciting world of reading!

Critter Riddles

Marilyn Helmer

Eric Parker

Kids Can Press

For Duncan William MacDonald — M.H.

Kids Can Read is a trademark of Kids Can Press

Text © 2003 Marilyn Helmer
Illustrations © 2003 Eric Parker

Kids Can Press acknowledges the financial support of the
Ontario Arts Council, the Canada Council for the Arts and
the Government of Canada, through the BPIDP, for our
publishing activity.

Published in Canada by   Published in the U.S. by
Kids Can Press Ltd.   Kids Can Press Ltd.
29 Birch Avenue   2250 Military Road
Toronto, ON M4V 1E2   Tonawanda, NY 14150

www.kidscanpress.com

Edited by David MacDonald
Designed by Marie Bartholomew

Printed and bound in Hong Kong, China, by Book Art Inc., Toronto

The hardcover edition of this book is smyth sewn casebound.
The paperback edition of this book is limp sewn with a
drawn-on cover.

CM 03 0 9 8 7 6 5 4 3 2 1
CM PA 03 0 9 8 7 6 5 4 3 2 1

National Library of Canada Cataloguing in Publication Data

Helmer, Marilyn
   Critter riddles / Marilyn Helmer ; illustrator, Eric Parker.

(Kids Can read)
ISBN 1-55337-445-2 (bound).   ISBN 1-55337-411-8 (pbk.)

1. Riddles, Juvenile. 2. Animals — Juvenile literature.
I. Parker, Eric II. Title. III. Series: Kids Can read (Toronto, Ont.)

PN6371.5.H44 2003   C818'.5402   C2002-901546-4

Kids Can Press is a *Corus*™ Entertainment company

What do you call a lion who never tells the truth?

The Lyin' King

What is the Three Little Pigs' favorite food?

Dill piggles

How do bees travel from place to place?

They take the buzz.

What should you do if you find a gorilla sleeping in your bed?

Go sleep in another bed.

What would you get if you crossed a rabbit with a frog?

Peter Ribbid

What is black and white and goes up and down?

A zebra on a seesaw

What do you call a brave chimpanzee?

A spunky monkey

When should you give your pet budgie
a present?

On his bird-day

Why do elephants like peanuts?

Because coconuts get stuck in their trunks

How do mice keep their breath smelling
fresh?

They use mouse-wash.

What is a boa constrictor's favorite game?

Snakes and Ladders

What did the boy bird call the girl bird?

His tweet-heart

How do eels get to the top of tall buildings?

They take an eel-evator.

How does a duckling get out of its egg?

He quacks it open.

How many sheep does it take to knit a scarf?

None – sheep can't knit.

What would you call a lazy kangaroo?

A pouch potato

What do two rhinoceroses do when they
meet on the road?

They honk their horns.

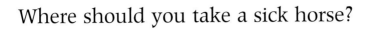

Where should you take a sick horse?

To the horse-pital, of course!

What game do moose like to play at parties?

Moose-ical chairs

What did the cat say when she got her tail caught in the door?

Me-owww!

What would you get if you met a grizzly in the woods?

A bear scare

What's big and gray and green and red and yellow and blue and black?

An elephant in a box of crayons

What do you get when you cross a squirrel with a peanut?

Something that climbs trees and acts like a nut

Which side of a tiger has the most stripes?

The outside

What do you call a dog who drives a sleigh and says, "Ho! Ho! Ho!"?

Santa Paws

What's black and white and red all over?

An embarrassed penguin

What do you call an insect who walks
around in tap shoes?

A clatter-pillar

How does a goose blow its nose?

With a honk-erchief

What kind of dolls do lambs like to play with?

Baa-bie dolls

What kind of stories do baby bears like best?

Furry tales